D0966443

THE JUNGLE BOOK

by RUDYARD KIPLING

#5 The Boy and His Sled Dog

Adapted by Diane Namm

Illustrated by Nathan Hale

STERLING

New York / London
www.sterlingpublishing.com/kids

STERLING and the distinctive Sterling logo are
registered trademarks of Sterling Publishing Co., Inc.

Library of Congress Cataloging-in-Publication Data Available

Lot #: 10   9   8   7   6   5   4   3   2   1
02/10
Published by Sterling Publishing Co., Inc.
387 Park Avenue South, New York, NY 10016
Text © 2010 by Sterling Publishing Co., Inc
Illustrations © 2010 by Nathan Hale
Distributed in Canada by Sterling Publishing
$^c/_o$ Canadian Manda Group, 165 Dufferin Street
Toronto, Ontario, Canada M6K 3H6
Distributed in the United Kingdom by GMC Distribution Services
Castle Place, 166 High Street, Lewes, East Sussex, England BN7 1XU
Distributed in Australia by Capricorn Link (Australia) Pty. Ltd.
P.O. Box 704, Windsor, NSW 2756, Australia

Printed in China
All rights reserved.

Sterling ISBN 978-1-4027-6723-4

For information about custom editions, special sales, premium and
corporate purchases, please contact Sterling Special Sales
Department at 800-805-5489 or specialsales@sterlingpublishing.com.

Contents

The Young Ones

In a cold and snowy
faraway place, there lived
a little Inuit boy
named Quiquern.
Quiquern wanted to drive
a sled so he could hunt
and fish like the older
boys in his village.

"I want to come with you,"
Quiquern said to a group of boys.
"I can hunt and fish as well as you!"
The boys just laughed.

"Father, I want to hunt and fish!"
said Quiquern.
"Son," his father said.
"You have much to learn if you
want to become a great hunter.
Here, this is for you."

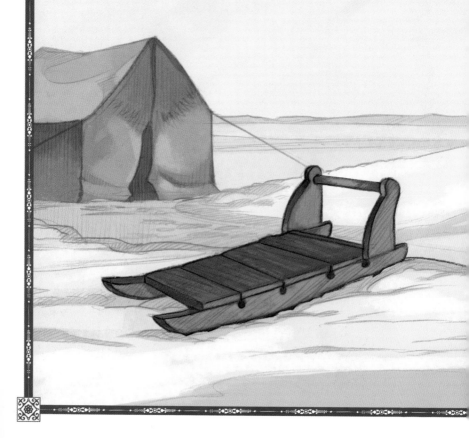

His father handed Quiquern
a small puppy and a sled,
just the right size for a boy.
Quiquern's face lit up.

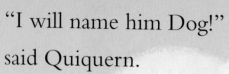

"I will name him Dog!"
said Quiquern.
"I will take care of him.
I will teach him to be the
best sled dog in the village."

Quiquern put the puppy on the sled
and gave him a ride.
Quinquern wanted Dog to know
just what to do when it was his turn
to pull the sled.

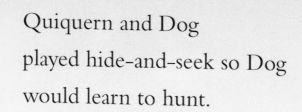

Quiquern and Dog
played hide-and-seek so Dog
would learn to hunt.

They played fetch,

so Dog would learn to fish.

At last, Dog was ready!

He could hunt and fish,

and he could pull Quiquern's sled.

"Father, watch me!" Quiquern called.

"Go, Dog, go!" he shouted.

Dog began to run.

Dog and the sled went one way.

Quiquern went the other!

"Some great hunter!" the
older boys laughed.

The Big Storm

Soon after, it began to snow.
At first, snowflakes drifted
down slowly from the sky.
Then the flakes came faster
and thicker until the whole
village was covered in a
frozen white blanket of snow.

There was more snow than
the villagers had ever seen.
The snow covered all the
houses and sleds.

The villagers tried to free their sleds
from the heavy ice and snow.
"Pull!" they shouted to the dogs.
"Push!" they yelled at each other.

For many days, they could not
move the sleds and could not
get out on the ice to fish.
The villagers were very hungry.

The Gray Wolf

"I can fish, Father!" Quiquern said.
"My sled is light.
The snow can't stop me."
"It is too far for you and Dog
to go alone," Father said.
"Let me try, Father, or everyone in
the village will starve,"
begged Quiquern.

Quiquern and Dog pushed
through the snow.
They needed to get to the holes
in the ice where they could fish.
When they were halfway there,
another snowstorm began.
Quiquern and Dog spent a
cold night in a cave.
But they were not afraid.
They had each other.

The next morning,
Quiquern and Dog woke up.
The air was filled with
blinding snow.
Quiquern did not know
which way to go!
Just then, they both heard
a low, scary growl.

"Wolf!" shouted Quiquern.
The hairs on Dog's back
stood up on end.
Dog bared his teeth
and gave a long, deep growl.
"Dog! No! Stay here!"
Quiquern cried out.

The wolf bared his teeth,
but Dog did not budge.
Dog stared at the wolf
for a long, long time
until the wolf finally backed
down and turned away.

The Big Fish

Meanwhile, the sun came out
and the snow stopped falling.
Quiquern was able to see the path
to the fishing holes in the ice.
"Run, Dog!" Quiquern shouted
as he jumped onto the sled.
Before long, Quiquern and Dog
were at the fishing holes.

Quiquern dropped his fishing
line down into a hole
the way he had seen his
father and the older boys do.

After a short time, Quiquern
felt a tug on his fishing line.
"A fish!" Quiquern called out.
The fish tugged harder . . .
and harder! It pulled
and pulled against Quiquern's line.
"Help me, Dog!" Quiquern cried.

Quiquern and Dog
tugged and pulled and
pulled and tugged until …
"We've got him!" Quiquern
shouted with glee.
The big fish flopped
onto the ice with a
great big plop!

Quiquern and Dog
returned to the village with a
fish big enough to feed everyone.
"Hurray for Quiquern,"
the villagers shouted.
Quiquern and Dog were heroes!
And from that day on, Quiquern was
always asked to join the hunting party.